Published by Scholastic Inc.
90 Old Sherman Turnpike, Danbury, Connecticut 06816.

For information regarding permission, write to:
Disney Licensed Publishing
114 Fifth Avenue, New York, New York 10011.

ISBN 0-7172-6803-9

Designed and produced by Bill SMITH STUDIO.

Printed in the U.S.A.
First printing, September 2003

The Sea Symphony

A Story About
Forgiveness

by **Annie Auerbach**
illustrated by
S.I. International

SCHOLASTIC INC.

New York   Toronto   London   Auckland   Sydney
Mexico City   New Delhi   Hong Kong   Buenos Aires

One afternoon, Princess Ariel was playing
tag with the twins when suddenly . . . CRASH!
They knocked over a beautiful sculpture.
Ariel and the twins gathered up the pieces and
quickly tried to put it back together before
her father found out.

"Ariel? Arista? Alana?" King Triton's voice boomed. "I'm home."

"No!" Ariel cried. "We haven't finished yet."

As soon as Triton came in, he noticed the broken sculpture.

"*A*riel!" Triton thundered. "What happened to this sculpture?" Scared of Triton, the twins fled.

"*I*'m sorry," Ariel said. "It was an accident. We were playing tag and—"

"How many times have I told you not to play tag in the palace?" Triton said. "You know the rules."

$\mathcal{A}$riel felt terrible. "I'm so sorry, Daddy. Will you please forgive me?"

Triton did forgive his daughter and then began to mend the sculpture. "Now go and play *outside* the palace."

"Yes, Daddy."

Soon after, as Ariel passed a cave, she heard the most beautiful sound. She swam over and found her sister Alana inside.

"Oh, Ariel," gushed Alana. "This is the best present! I simply love this . . . this . . . what did you call it?"

"Scuttle called it a pitsytooter," Ariel said.

"*I* want to play it at the Sea Symphony this weekend," Alana said, "instead of singing my solo." The Sea Symphony was held once a year. Merfolk and sea creatures from all the world's oceans gathered to take part in it.

"But you know Daddy forbids us to have human objects," Ariel said, thinking about her own secret collection. "How could you show it in public?"

"*I* think once he hears how well I play at the symphony, he'll change his mind," said Alana. "I'm just going to sneak it in with my things."

$\mathcal{A}$riel smiled. "Well, I'm sure it will make my first time at the Sea Symphony a memorable one!" Ariel was finally old enough to attend the famous celebration. "See you later," she called to her sister as she swam away. "I have to pack!"

$\mathcal{T}$o get to the symphony by Saturday, the merfolk of Atlantica had to travel a great distance. On Friday, preparations began for the journey.

King Triton announced that each of his daughters would ride with him for a portion of the journey. Alana was to be first. "Get your bag and join me up front," Triton told her.

When Alana went to her room, she saw the pitsytooter and panicked. What if her father discovered it as she rode next to him? So Alana hid the pitsytooter inside Ariel's bag. "I can get it out later," she thought.

$\mathcal{A}$lana left the room, just as her sisters filed in to pick up their bags. But on Ariel's way out, her bag opened up and the pitsytooter rolled out . . . landing right in front of Triton!

"What is this?" Triton said, bending over to pick it up. "Is this a human object?"

"But, Daddy, it's not—" Ariel interrupted.

"*A*riel, I'm very disappointed in you,"
Triton replied. "You must learn from this. You're
grounded and you cannot go to the Sea Symphony."

$\mathcal{A}$riel looked over at Alana. "She must have put it in my bag," Ariel thought. "But why?"

Alana just looked down, not offering to help her sister and tell the truth. "I never dreamed this would happen," Alana thought.

$\mathcal{B}$efore long, the sea horses set off with
a splash.

Ariel swam to her room. "I'll never forgive
Alana for this!" she declared. That evening, she
cried herself to sleep.

Very early the next morning, Ariel was woken up by Alana.

"What are you doing here?" Ariel asked, as she got out of bed and swam out of the room.

"*A*riel!" called Alana, following her. "I came back to apologize."

But Ariel wouldn't listen—or even stop to hear what her sister had to say.

"*I*'m so sorry I put the pitsytooter in your bag," Alana said. "When Daddy wanted me to ride next to him, I panicked. I was afraid he'd find out about the pitsytooter before he heard me play it at the symphony."

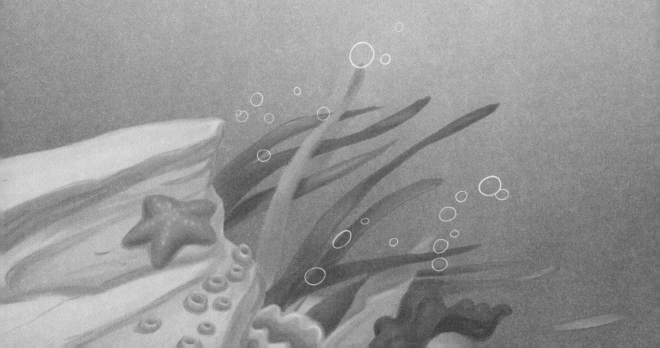

"So why did you come back?" Ariel asked.

"I felt terrible, so I told Daddy everything. He arranged for a sea horse to bring me back here so that I could work things out with you. Oh, please forgive me," Alana pleaded.

Just then Ariel swam past the sculpture—the same one she had knocked over the day before.

*W*hat would a princess do?

$\mathcal{A}$riel remembered how her father had forgiven her. She knew she must do the same with Alana.

"Okay, Alana," Ariel said, "I forgive you."

Alana threw her arms around Ariel in a big hug.

Suddenly Alana broke away from the embrace. "Ariel, you must get going," she said. "I don't want you to miss the symphony."

"*I*'m only going if you come with me," Ariel said.

"No," said Alana. "I don't deserve to go."

"I've forgiven you, now forgive yourself," Ariel said. "Besides, it wouldn't be the same without you there."

Alana agreed, and the two sisters took off for
the Sea Symphony. They arrived just as the
overture was beginning.

*T*riton smiled when he saw them swim in arm in arm.

"This music sounds better than any human object could make, don't you think?" Alana whispered to her sister.

Ariel nodded and whispered back, "And it sounds best when I can share it with you!"

The End